The Pied Piper

A Tale about Promises

Retold by Tom DeFalco
Illustrated by Joe Ewers

Famous Fables

Reader's Digest Young Families

Once upon a time there was a town called Hamelin, and it sat on the banks of a great river. It was a happy and cozy little town until a large group of rats moved in.

The rats were very naughty. They climbed into cupboards and ate the food. They made nests in old dresser drawers and chewed on clothes. They played loudly at night, so no one could get a wink of sleep.

The townspeople complained to the mayor.

"Cats will solve our problem," the mayor said.
He gathered up as many cats as he could find and
released them into the streets.

The mayor's plan did not work. The rats were
too strong and clever. They banded together and
chased the cats out of town.

The mayor was desperate. He needed a new
plan. "I must hire a professional rat catcher," he said.
"I will pay one hundred bags of gold to anyone who
can get rid of these rats."

Rat catchers came to Hamelin from across
the land. Some brought strange potions and special
traps. Others came with unusual pets to hunt the rats.

All of these rat catchers failed!

The mayor didn't know what to do. Then a strange
young man arrived in Hamelin. He was dressed in
colorful clothes and wore a long feather in his hat.
He carried a simple flute.

"I am the Pied Piper," the young man said. "If you
promise to pay me one hundred bags of gold, I will
get rid of all your rats."

After the mayor agreed to pay him, the young man slowly walked through the town and started to play his flute. The rats heard the music, and they were soon scampering out of their nests. They all gathered behind the Pied Piper and began to dance.

The Pied Piper led the rats to a distant meadow in the mountains. There they found plants to eat and holes for nests. The rats decided to settle in the meadow, which was a perfect place for them to live.

The Pied Piper returned to Hamelin. He asked for his hundred bags of gold, but the mayor laughed at him. "All you did was play a flute," the mayor said. "I will give you one bag of gold and not a penny more."

"Very well," the Pied Piper said as he sadly walked away. "But you should have kept your promise."

The mayor was feeling quite proud of himself.
The town no longer had rats, and he had saved
ninety-nine bags of gold.

But the mayor had not heard the last of the Pied
Piper. The young man returned to Hamelin early the
next morning and began to play his flute. All of the
children in the town quickly scrambled out of their
beds. Dancing and laughing, the children joined
hands and followed the Pied Piper out of Hamelin.

The Pied Piper led the children into a lovely green forest. They laughed, played party games and sang happy songs long into the night.

But the people of Hamelin were not happy. They missed their children and complained to the mayor.

"This is all your fault," they said. "We want our children back."

The mayor begged the Pied Piper to return the children of Hamelin. "If you do," the mayor said to him, "I will give you the hundred bags of gold I promised you."

"People who break promises must pay for not keeping their word," the Pied Piper said. "The price is now two hundred bags of gold."

The mayor almost fainted when he heard the new price. But he knew that he had been wrong, and so he paid the piper.

The sound of laughter filled the streets of Hamelin as the Pied Piper led the children back into the little town. The people of Hamelin were so grateful to the Pied Piper that they arranged a large celebration in his honor.

Everyone in the town of Hamelin lived happily ever after, including the mayor. He had learned an important lesson, and he never broke another promise.

Famous Fables, Lasting Virtues

Tips for Parents

Now that you've read The Pied Piper, *use these pages as a guide in teaching your child the virtues in the story. By talking about the story and engaging in the suggested activities, you can help your child develop good judgment and a strong moral character.*

About Promises

The best way for children to learn about making and keeping promises is for parents to be good role models. If you keep the promises you make, your child will too. In addition, your child will trust you and, in turn, will feel that you trust him.

1. *Be sure you'll be able to keep the promises you make to your child.* Be aware that children interpret some general statements, such as "I have to buy just one thing in the grocery store and then we'll go," as promises. Avoid promising something in the future as a reward for good behavior in the present, hoping your child will forget about it. ("You can't play at your friend's house today. . .maybe next week sometime.") Kids have very good memories when it comes to promises. If you find you can't keep a promise, always explain why.

2. *Avoid unreasonable or false promises.* Children often know from the start when a promise is false, such as "This shot won't hurt, I promise." Being accurate and truthful will strengthen the bonds of trust between you and your child.

3. *Set goals that are appropriate for your child's age.* It's easier to succeed in keeping a promise when the promise is reasonable. Always acknowledge your child's achievement in keeping a promise by praising him, however small the promise or task may seem.

4. *Teach the difference between keeping promises and keeping secrets.* Make clear to your child that a promise to keep a secret is different from other types of promises. Such secrets are often hurtful or harmful and best told to a loving parent. Things that are surprises— gifts for birthdays, a visit from a favorite relative—should be called *surprises*, not *secrets*.